OTHER YEARLING BOOKS YOU WILL ENJOY:

YEARLING BOOKS/YOUNG YEARLINGS/YEARLING CLASSICS are designed especially to entertain and enlighten young people. Patricia Reilly Giff, consultant to this series, received her bachelor's degree from Marymount College and a master's degree in history from St. John's University. She holds a Professional Diploma in Reading and a Doctorate of Humane Letters from Hofstra University. She was a teacher and reading consultant for many years, and is the author of numerous books for young readers.

In the midst of the world's corruption,
A heart of pure white jade.

MIEKO and the
Fifth Treasure

ELEANOR COERR

CALLIGRAPHY BY
CECIL H. UYEHARA

A Yearling Book

The author wishes to acknowledge Mr. Terumasa Matsunaga, of Nagasaki, for his valuable and generous assistance in reading the manuscript for accuracy.

Special thanks to Mr. Cecil Uyehara for his expertise and artistry, and to my editor, Kate Gallagher, for her caring attention.

Published by
Bantam Doubleday Dell Books for Young Readers
a division of
Bantam Doubleday Dell Publishing Group, Inc.
1540 Broadway
New York, New York 10036

ISBN: 0-440-40947-0

Reprinted by arrangement with The Putnam & Grosset Group, on behalf of G. P. Putnam's Sons

Printed in the United States of America

September 1994

10   9

To the children of Nagasaki

CONTENTS

ONE

MIEKO

"Mieko, come down to breakfast!" Grandma's cheery voice floated up from the kitchen. "It's time you got out of bed."

But Mieko was not in bed. She was sitting very still and feeling very sorry for herself.

"In a minute," she called back.

Mieko stared at the art supplies lined up on the red

lacquer chest. Her art teacher, Mr. Araki, had called them "the four treasures." There was a fine sable brush, an inkstick, an inkstone shaped like a lily pond, and a roll of rice paper. Mieko had used them to paint Japanese word-pictures. Calligraphy was what she liked to do more than anything else in the world.

Mr. Araki had also told her, "Mieko, you are one of the lucky few who are born with the fifth treasure—beauty in the heart. When you paint, that beauty flows from your heart to your hand, to the brush, and out onto the paper. With lots of practice, you will surely become a great artist."

Mieko didn't really understand what beauty in the heart meant, but she knew that she was never so happy as when she had a brush in her hand, with every stroke getting better.

Mieko sighed. She thought about how wonderful it had been to sit alone in her room and paint. She used to weave brushstrokes, curves, and dots into word-pictures that seemed to have a life of their own. Her two black strokes for "man" looked like two legs striding across the fields. She could almost hear the raindrops in her word-picture for "rain." When she painted, she was in a magical world.

10

But everything was different now.

She would never forget the day when The Thunderbolt—the atom bomb—was dropped on Nagasaki, sending shock waves out to her town. It was like the end of the world. Windows shattered and roof tiles flew through the air. Mieko was knocked to the ground. When she had put up an arm to shield her face, a jagged piece of glass had torn into her hand, ripping a deep gash from her fingers to the wrist. Blood was everywhere. Now, two weeks later, the wound still throbbed painfully underneath the bandage.

"Nothing serious," Father had said in his soothing doctor's voice. "Your hand will heal quickly and you will soon be painting again."

Mieko did not believe him. The wound looked awful. And her hand was useless. Besides, she had seen many around her with worse injuries, and Father had told them "nothing serious," too. He said that to make his patients feel better.

And now she had been shipped to Grandpa's farm.

"Just for a few months, Mieko," Mother had explained, forcing a smile. "We must remain here to take care of the injured. Besides, the fresh air and farm food will be good for you."

Mieko wanted to stay home. She was bitter about leaving her parents. She was bitter about leaving her friends. She was frightened about going to a new school. And she hated the horrible bomb that had ruined everything.

"With all the bitterness and hate inside of me," she thought, "there isn't room for any beauty." The fifth treasure was gone.

"Breakfast is waiting, Mieko!" Grandma called again.

Mieko gave a quick brush to her bangs and went downstairs.

She sat at the low table and tried to pick up her chopsticks. When they fell with a clatter, Grandma picked them up and fed Mieko as though she were a little baby. Her plump face wreathed in smiles, Grandma poked food into Mieko's mouth, then carefully wiped her chin.

"Good food cures everything," Grandma said.

Mieko did not mind the attention, especially when she felt so sorry for herself.

"My!" Grandma gave Mieko's arm a little pinch. "You are as thin as a young bamboo. We saved this special white rice for an important occasion like having you here with us. You must eat every grain."

Mieko remembered that Mother always called it "silver rice." She felt a wave of homesickness. Tears stung her eyes and she could hardly swallow.

Grandma put her arms around Mieko and rocked her back and forth. "Hush, hush!" she crooned. "You are just tired from that long train ride yesterday."

"You will feel better tomorrow," said Grandpa.

Mieko hung her head, knowing that they did not understand. How could tomorrow be better? She would never paint word-pictures again, and she would never feel the joy of having the fifth treasure. She would hear the bomb over and over again, and know that things at home would never be the same.

After supper they all had baths in the backyard tub and put on cotton kimonos. Then they sat outside to enjoy the evening breeze. Twilight fell and crickets began to sing. Mieko thought they sounded sad.

Grandpa pointed to a large rock in the tiny garden behind the house.

"See that?" he said proudly. "Last year I hauled it down the mountain in the cart. Mieko, can you read the words carved into my rock?"

Mieko studied the strokes that formed the word-pictures, but they were difficult to make out. She shook her head.

" 'Spilled water never returns to the glass,' " Grandpa explained. "It means that one should not worry about things that cannot be changed."

He paused to puff on his cigarette. Then he went on, "Like Japan losing the war. Like all that has been lost or hurt by the bomb." And glancing quickly at Mieko, "Like your hand being injured, and your parents sending you to us."

Grandma smiled, patting Mieko's shoulder. "I know it's not easy for a ten-year-old to understand, but you must try."

Mieko blinked back the tears. She did not want to understand. The only thing she wanted was to be back home, with everything like it was before.

At bedtime Grandma laid out a futon and hung a mosquito net over it for Mieko.

When she saw the four treasures on top of the chest, Grandma nodded approvingly. "I see that you did not forget your calligraphy supplies. Good. You will soon be practicing again."

"No, I won't!" Mieko burst out. She shoved the four treasures into a drawer. "The bomb spoiled everything, Grandma. I'll never, never paint again."

"Don't talk like that," Grandma said, flustered. "Your hand will get better . . ."

"But my fingers will always be stiff and awkward like dried-up shrimp," Mieko said in a small voice. "And my brushstrokes will look like sticks."

She threw herself onto the futon and pulled the sheet up over her head.

Grandma sighed.

"I'll write to your parents and tell them that you arrived safely," she said, turning out the light. "Good-night."

It was the first time Mieko had ever been away from home alone. She longed for her own bedroom, where her teacher's painting hung on the wall and Mother's peach tree rustled its leaves outside her window.

What if something happened to Mother and Father? What if they got sick and died? What if she never saw them again? Finally, exhausted, Mieko stuffed a pillow against her mouth and cried herself to sleep.

That night she had a nightmare. A plane was droning overhead and then a big bomb exploded in her face. Mieko woke up screaming.

Grandpa knelt by the futon.

"The war is over now," he said, putting his arms around her. "There are no more bombs."

But Mieko could not stop the sobs shaking her whole body.

"Shh—shh! You must stop crying," Grandpa whispered. "Your tears will not help those who were killed by the atom bomb. Their souls must swim across the River of Death to heaven. Every tear you shed drops into the river and makes it deeper."

Mieko shuddered, imagining what it would be like to struggle in that icy cold water. Gradually, she became quiet.

Grandpa straightened the bedclothes.

"Enough of dreary thoughts," he said. "Try to sleep like my rock in the garden."

As soon as he was gone Mieko went to the open window. She pushed up her bangs, letting the night air cool her damp forehead. With no moonlight Mieko could barely see Grandpa's rock. She was sorry for it, so awfully alone out there in the swallowing dark. It looked as alone as she felt.

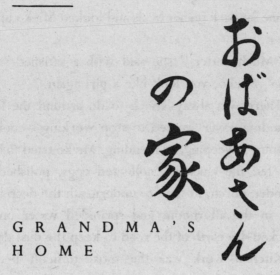

TWO

GRANDMA'S HOME

Every morning Mieko put on the dress that Grandma had sewn out of an old summer cotton kimono. It had no buttons or belt so that Mieko could easily slip it over her head. Grandma had taken the long-sleeved blouses and baggy trousers that Mieko had brought and put them into the scrapbag.

"I don't understand why the government made

girls wear those hot, prickly outfits," she said. "Thank goodness the war is over and you can put on decent clothes again."

She sat back on her heels and looked Mieko up and down.

"Much better," she said with a satisfied smile. "Yes, Mieko, you look like a girl again."

There was always much to do around the farm. Grandma never seemed to stop working—cooking, cleaning, sweeping, or mending. Mieko tried to help. She fed the chickens, collected eggs, polished the wooden porch, lit the fire underneath the deep bathtub in the afternoon, and sprinkled water on the cracked dry earth of the road to keep the dust down.

Kitchen work was the most difficult because Mieko's hand was clumsy and it hurt whenever she tried to hold a knife or spoon. She took a long time slicing eggplants and cucumbers with her left hand.

Once Mieko dropped a whole dish of chopped fish onto the floor. She stood there looking down at the mess, biting her lip.

"I'm not good for anything!" she cried.

Grandma scooped up the fish, talking all the while.

"Never mind, Mieko. It's just a little thing. When the doctor came last week he said that your hand will soon be as good as new. Then you will have no more accidents.''

Mieko was silent. She knew it would never be as good as new.

As the summer days dragged on, Mieko worried more and more about school. Her grandparents had not mentioned it, and she hoped that they had forgotten.

But one muggy September morning when they were eating rice and miso soup, Grandma calmly said, "Mieko, you will be going to school next week.''

Mieko almost dropped the porcelain spoon that she was trying to carry to her mouth. She was not hungry any more.

For several moments there were only the sounds of a farm morning—hens clucking and birds scolding in the garden.

Grandma and Grandpa exchanged worried glances.

"You must go to school," Grandpa said. "It is important to keep up with your studies.''

Mieko knew all that. But a strange school? With children she did not know? And with a hideous, twisted hand?

19

"Maybe they won't like me," she said in a low voice.

"Not like you!" Grandma's bright eyes sent off sparks. "Why would the others not like you? You are a nice girl with good manners and new clothes." And she brought out a school uniform, neatly sewn and pressed.

"Here!" She handed it to Mieko. "I made it for a surprise. Go try it on."

Mieko did not like that kind of surprise. Trembling, she slowly pulled on the navy skirt and white blouse that smelled of camphor.

"I saved these pieces of cloth all through the war," Grandma said, giving the skirt a tug to straighten it. She beamed. "A perfect fit."

Mieko lowered her eyes. "Thank you, Grandma," she murmured.

The first day of school arrived. That morning, Mieko came into the kitchen, looking a little pale.

"I think I'm getting some kind of germ," she said, coughing. "My throat is sore. I think I'm coming down with mumps."

"Open your mouth and say ahhhh," Grandma said in her no-nonsense voice.

She held Mieko's tongue down with a spoon and peered inside. Then she felt Mieko's neck.

"Your throat is fine, and your glands are not even the tiniest bit swollen."

"Do I have to go today?" Mieko pleaded. "Do I, Grandma?"

Grandma paid no attention. She continued stuffing rice into beancurd envelopes that looked like fat sails. Then she packed them neatly into a lunchbox.

"Such heat!" she said, dabbing at her neck with the edge of her apron. "Mieko, don't walk too fast this morning."

"I don't even know where the school is," Mieko said. "And . . . and I might get lost."

"I will take you there on my way to the field," Grandpa interrupted. "Now scoot upstairs and get ready."

"Don't forget your art supplies," Grandma called, putting a piece of dried fish into the lunchbox for a treat.

Mieko thought it was silly to bring the four treasures when she was not going to use them. But to please Grandma, she stuck them into her black leather schoolbag.

She took such a long time getting ready that

Grandpa finally stomped upstairs. Mieko was combing her hair and fussing with her uniform.

"Come on!" he said firmly. "You don't want to be late on your first day."

"It is the first day that is so scary," Mieko wailed. "I will sit in the wrong seat . . . say the wrong things . . . and everyone will stare at my hand."

Mieko thought that the new puckered red skin looked even worse than the scabs that were coming off.

But there was no escape. She trudged alongside Grandpa to school, clutching his work-roughened hand all the way. When they got there, she hung back.

"Go on in," Grandpa said, giving her a gentle push. "You will be all right."

Mieko watched him stride away until he turned the corner. For an instant she stood there, paralyzed with fear. Then she took a long, shaky breath and walked slowly through the doorway.

THREE

S C H O O L

Mieko slipped out of her geta and put them in one of the shoe boxes in the hall. She wiped her moist hands on her skirt and shifted from one foot to the other, waiting for a teacher to come along and direct her to the right classroom. She pictured her teacher looking old and mean.

Out of the corner of her eye Mieko saw the students come in, some laughing, some arm-in-arm.

They had lived in the town all their lives and knew each other well. Nobody spoke to Mieko.

It was a pleasant surprise when a pretty young woman introduced herself.

"You must be Mieko," the teacher said warmly. "Your grandfather told me about you. I am Miss Suzuki."

After bowing politely, Mieko followed Miss Suzuki into the classroom to a desk near the back. She gave Mieko a stubby pencil, carefully sharpened at both ends, and some pages of an old newspaper.

"Try to write in the white spaces," Miss Suzuki said. "I hope we will be getting more supplies now that the war is over. Until then, we must make do."

As Mieko looked around at all the unsmiling faces, she knew more than ever what loneliness meant.

"We have a new pupil," the teacher announced. "Mieko, please stand up."

Her knees shaking, Mieko got to her feet as thirty pairs of eyes gazed at her. She blushed and tried to hide her hand behind her back.

"Let's make her feel welcome," Miss Suzuki went on. "She has just come from a town near Nagasaki, and I expect all of you to help her get acquainted with our school."

This caused a buzzing in the room. As Mieko sank back into her chair, she heard whispers.

"That's where the big bomb exploded . . . Look at her hand . . . It makes me sick."

Mieko felt smaller than a fly. Just because no bombs had dropped on this part of Japan was no reason to be stupid. She wanted to scream "Stupid!" at them all. But she swallowed the word. Mother had often warned her that a nasty word was like a bird— once it flew out of her mouth it would never fly back. Micko pressed her lips together so that the word could not escape.

During the morning, Mieko tried hard to concentrate, but Akira made it impossible. He was a skinny boy with stiff short hair that stood up like a brush and he wore black-rimmed glasses.

Whenever Miss Suzuki was not looking, Akira turned around and made faces at Mieko. He crossed his eyes and twisted his mouth into strange shapes. He looked so silly that Mieko almost laughed. But when he hissed, "Monster-hand!" she glared at him.

Mieko heard her mother saying, "Always see beauty, never see ugliness." How could anyone see beauty in Akira?

It seemed that the morning would never end. Mieko was so nervous that she stumbled over her own feet and twice she dropped her book. In history class, she could not remember all the names of the Japanese emperors. Everyone knew those. She did not even try to write, but kept her hands folded in her lap.

During arithmetic, there was a sudden loud noise outside, and Mieko ducked underneath the desk. Almost the moment she did it she felt silly. It was only a truck backfiring, not a bomb exploding. Still, she was shaking. When Akira and some of the others tittered, Mieko wanted to die on the spot.

At that moment Miss Suzuki was pointing to a giant abacus that stood in front of the room.

"Mieko," she was saying, "please come up and work out this problem in multiplication."

"I . . . I didn't hear the question," Mieko stammered, her mouth dry.

Miss Suzuki's voice was disapproving.

"You really must try to pay attention, Mieko."

Akira went up to the abacus and quickly moved the counters to get the correct answer. On the way back to his seat he gave Mieko a smug look and stuck out his tongue.

"I hope your tongue falls off!" Mieko muttered under her breath.

By lunchtime Mieko's stomach was in knots. She couldn't eat one bite of the rice and fish that Grandma had prepared for her. She just sat there, staring at her chopsticks. How could she use them in front of the others? What if she dropped food all over the place? Wouldn't Akira like that!

As they filed out into the schoolyard, Akira came up behind Mieko and grabbed her schoolbag. He dug into it and pulled out her painting brush. In a flash, he swaggered out into the yard shouting, "Hey! Look what I've got! Monster-hand's dirty old atom bomb brush!"

Mieko turned pale and ran after him, trying to grab her brush.

"Give it back!" she screamed. "It's mine!"

Other boys joined in the game.

"Monster-hand! Monster-hand!" they chanted, tossing the brush from one to the other, always just out of Mieko's reach.

She felt like crying, but she gritted her teeth, not wanting to cry in front of them.

Suddenly she heard a girl's voice.

"Stop that! You're acting like a bunch of babies."

———

That ended the trouble. Akira threw the brush to Mieko. The boys shrugged and walked away.

The girl handed Mieko her bag and said, "Don't let those dumb boys bother you! They are always doing something childish."

Mieko knew the girl was called Yoshi. She was small and dainty with a red bow in her hair. And she smelled of flowers. Mieko wished that she could be exactly like her—so calm and pretty. Instead, she was upset and hot and sweaty. She was a freak with an ugly hand that seemed to stick out a mile.

Soon a group of girls had gathered around, staring curiously at Mieko and asking questions.

"Did you get that scar from the bomb? What was it like? Were there lots of dead bodies? What did they look like?"

Mieko looked from one to another. She felt hot and dizzy and her legs went rubbery. All at once the ring of faces around her started melting together, and she crumpled to the ground. The girls—suddenly quiet—backed away.

F O U R

G R A N D P A

When Mieko came to, she heard voices. The principal was speaking to Miss Suzuki.

"She just seems to be overexcited, that's all."

"What makes it so sad," Miss Suzuki said, "is that a few children have been teasing her. As if she hasn't been through enough."

Mieko sat up and drank some water. All she wanted now was to get out of there.

"Do you think you can walk home alone?" Miss

Suzuki's voice was concerned. "I can send one of the students with you."

"No, thank you!" Mieko said quickly. "I'm fine now."

She certainly did not want any help from them. And if Grandma knew about the fainting spell, she would make a fuss and call the doctor.

Mieko left the school. But instead of going straight home, she slowly walked to the field. Grandpa was working up to his hips in rice plants that were turning a golden brown. Mieko stood on the path, kicking up little clouds of dirt until he saw her and came over.

"Phew!" he exclaimed, tipping back his straw hat and wiping his forehead with a small towel. "Autumn is late this year. I'll be glad when it cools off."

Mieko noticed how much his tanned face was like Father's—yet different. It was thinner and more wrinkled, and Grandpa's hair was gray.

"How was school?" Grandpa asked, tucking the small towel back into his belt.

"Awful!" Mieko mumbled. "I hate everyone there."

Grandpa gave her a quick glance that seemed to see right into Mieko's mind.

"That is a heavy load of hate for a little girl to carry around." He rubbed the bony knuckles of his hands to ease the arthritis. "Of course they are all monsters?"

"Yes!" Mieko replied.

"Have you tried to be friends with anyone?"

Mieko thought of Yoshi. She shrugged and kept her head down so that she wouldn't have to meet his eyes.

Grandpa swept an arm toward the rice field.

"See that? Rice does not grow all by itself. I must plant the seeds, fertilize them, and see that no weeds stop their growth. Then I must separate the seedlings and plant them farther apart. It is not easy." His face was serious. "It is not easy to make friends either, especially when you hate almost everyone."

Then he stretched and started back toward the field.

"Think about it!" he called over his shoulder.

Mieko was too upset to think about his words. She wasn't interested in growing rice, anyway.

At the house a shock was waiting for her. Inside the entrance, neatly placed together on the cement floor—toes out—were two shiny brown shoes.

———

Mieko tried to slip past the living room, but Grandma heard her.

"There you are!" she said. "We have been waiting for you. Come in and say hello to Miss Suzuki."

Mieko sighed and stepped up into the room. She knelt on the tatami, and bowed her head in greeting. She wondered what Miss Suzuki wanted.

Grandma poured some tea for Mieko into one of her best cups. Mieko noticed the flower design—the same as on Mother's dishes.

"Miss Suzuki thinks that you should stay home for a little while until you have your strength back," Grandma said.

The teacher nodded.

"When you feel better, Mieko, you may come back to us. You are always welcome." She gave Grandma a sideways glance. "There is plenty of time."

Mieko watched them over the rim of her cup.

Grandma frowned, tucking a wisp of gray hair into the bun at the back. "But Mieko must learn to get along with other children. And there is her painting . . ."

Miss Suzuki leaned forward and lowered her voice.

———

"Please don't worry. Mieko will be back in school soon and she can easily catch up. Of course, there is no reason why she cannot continue her painting at home."

Mieko's face lit up. No more school! No more teasing from Akira and the boys. No more giggles behind her back. Maybe she would never go back to that school. But continue with her painting? How could she do that? Without the fifth treasure it didn't matter.

Later that day, the mailman brought a letter from Mother.

Dear Mieko,

There are so many patients that your father and I are working long hours in the clinic. We hope that you are happy on the farm and getting strong and healthy. By now you must be in school and making many new friends. Write to us when you can. We miss you.

Love,
Mother

"Any news from home?" Grandma asked.

Mieko shook her head. Then she ran upstairs and put the letter away.

That night she was already in bed when Grandpa came home late. His footsteps sounded heavy and tired on the stairs.

"Mieko," he whispered, "are you still awake?"

She squeezed her eyes shut and pretended to be asleep. Mieko didn't want to hear any more about growing rice or making friends.

"I understand," Grandpa said, as if he knew that she was faking. "When the time is right, you will go back to school."

The kindness in his voice made Mieko feel worse. She lay very still, scarcely breathing.

At the door Grandpa said softly, "Believe me, Mieko, some lovely sunny day you will look around and find a friend. And in your happiness you will paint beautiful word-pictures again. Just like before."

Mieko heard the rustle of the door sliding shut.

"He's wrong," she thought. "I've lost the fifth treasure for good. And I'll never be happy again."

FIVE

WAITING

Grandma asked nothing of Mieko now. Long before Mieko woke up she would put on her black cotton work pants and shirt, cover her head with a straw hat, and be out in the fields to help Grandpa. He needed help because so many young men had gone to fight in the war and had never come back.

Days were just plain dull, like strips of dried old

seaweed. Mieko escaped into her thoughts, building a wall around herself the way a turtle builds its shell. She was always looking back, thinking about home.

Sometimes she scolded the hens to keep them from pecking holes in the paper panes of the sliding doors. Or she watched spiders spin their webs between the rocks underneath the porch. Mieko was like the snail that lumbered slowly toward the shade. Trapped inside and silent.

She would sit on the springy tatami in the living room for hours, studying the scroll painting in the alcove. Grandma changed it with the seasons, so this one showed trees in fall colors, and a poem written with graceful strokes.

> *I thought I saw the fluttering leaves arise,*
> *Returning to their branches;*
> *No, it was only butterflies!*

Before long, Mieko had memorized the calligraphy and could make a copy of it in her head. She remembered when her own brushstrokes had been good enough to hang on the wall.

Mieko avoided talking with anyone. The few times when Grandma had afternoon tea with a friend, Mieko would escape to the nearby beach. Someone had left a length of huge clay sewer pipe there, and its cool, shadowy interior was her secret hideaway. On the sandy floor she scratched out word-pictures with a stick—Mother, Father, and Home.

The sunshine was sparkling on the blue ocean, fishermen were hanging and mending their nets, sand crabs were skittering across the shore, and sea birds were swooping down for their dinner. But Mieko saw none of it. She couldn't see anything but her own loneliness.

Another letter arrived from Mother, this time for Grandpa and Grandma. Mieko leaned over Grandpa's shoulder as he read parts of it aloud. Mother said they were planning to come to the farm after the New Year holidays and take Mieko home.

Mieko's spirits sank. New Year's Day seemed like years away instead of just a few months.

There was a special note at the end for her:

Mieko dear, is your hand still very painful? By now you must be writing with a pencil. How is the brush-painting coming along? You haven't yet told us about school. Write soon.

Love,
Mother.

———

Mieko did not dare look at Grandpa and Grandma. She was ashamed. How could she write about school? Or new friends? Or painting? A lump came into her throat and she ran outside. Leaning against the side of the house, Mieko could hear voices from the living room.

"That girl keeps too much to herself." Grandma sounded anxious. "It is as though a wicked goblin has taken over her soul. She hardly smiles, and whenever anyone drops in, Mieko disappears as fast as a boiled egg slips off chopsticks. And she will not pick up a brush—or even a pencil."

Grandpa spoke calmly. "When she is ready, Mieko will go back to school."

After a long silence, he added, "A young girl in trouble should be left alone. Only Mieko can heal her inner self. We cannot do that for her."

"I suppose so," Grandma said with a deep sigh.

Mieko swallowed hard. She was making her grandparents unhappy, too.

In the morning the doctor arrived. He was surprised at the change in Mieko.

"My goodness, you don't look at all like the skinny girl who arrived in August. The farm food must do you good." He leaned toward Mieko. "But

I don't like that long face. A little happiness would help you grow up into a pretty young lady.''

Mieko blushed and managed a tiny smile.

"That's better," he said, touching her hand and moving the fingers. "Now, you should be painting and writing to loosen up those stiff muscles.''

"Is she all right?" asked Grandma, coming in from the kitchen, still carrying the radish she was chopping up for pickles. "Can she go back to school?''

He nodded and got up to leave.

Mieko's eyes moved from one to the other. The tightness in her throat almost choked her.

"But I never want to go back!''

"Never is a long, long time," the doctor said, his eyebrows drawn together in a frown. "You have a good mind, Mieko, and a talent for calligraphy. They will not develop if you stay home and sulk.''

"Nobody sees my mind." Mieko's voice trembled. "They see only my ugly hand. And I am not sulking.''

"I don't know what to do with her," Grandma said helplessly.

When the doctor spoke, his voice was stern.

"Mieko, you can be a bitter person all your life, but you are only hurting yourself and your family.

———

39

Hatred will grow in your heart like a bad weed until there is no room for love or beauty."

"I don't care!" Mieko shouted, running out the door.

Tears stinging her eyes, she ran past the quiet neighborhood farmhouses and climbed up the mountain. The path wound around oddly shaped rocks and over grassy slopes. Mieko did not stop until she reached a stream partway up. Hot and tired, she flopped down and dabbled her fingers in the cool water.

The air was quiet and dry as a rice cracker. Mieko rested her head on the mossy bank, listening to the slow droning of insects and the trickling of the water over pebbles.

Suddenly, there was a rustling nearby.

It was a queer sound—not very far from her. Mieko remembered the stories she had heard about the red-faced Tengu, the demon that lived in mountains. It was said that he had wings and claws and a long, long nose. He carried bad children into his cave and they were never seen again.

If that were true, Mieko thought, the Tengu would get her for sure. She began to think that perhaps she had been a little bad lately. Mieko counted the bad things: she worried her grandparents, stayed home from school, was rude to the doctor, hated almost everyone, and did not even try to paint or write a letter home. It was quite a lot.

Mieko held her breath and listened.

The spooky sound came again—a sort of whirring of wings.

She scrambled to her feet and scurried down the twisty path as fast as her legs could go.

SIX

YOSHI

As Mieko rushed headlong down the mountain she almost bumped into someone.

It was Yoshi.

In a yellow dress and matching bow in her black hair, Yoshi looked like a butterfly. For a few seconds Mieko was too stunned to say anything.

"What's the matter?" Yoshi asked. "Why are you running? You look scared to death."

When Mieko could get her breath, she pointed toward the mountain. "Up there," she panted, "near the stream. A Tengu was chasing me."

"Are you sure?" Yoshi asked, her eyes full of smiles. "We have no Tengu around here. At least, I don't think so."

Mieko's cheeks turned pink.

"I . . . I honestly did hear something."

"Probably some small animal." Yoshi looked curiously at Mieko. "Why don't you come to school anymore?"

"The doctor told Grandma that I needed a rest," Mieko said softly.

"We thought that you didn't like any of us at school."

"But I thought . . ." stammered Mieko, "I thought you might not like me."

An awkward silence fell between them.

Finally, Mieko said, "Well . . . I guess I should be getting back home."

Yoshi nodded and followed Mieko down the mountain. When they came to Mieko's yard, Grandma was sliding clothes off the bamboo clothesline into a basket.

"Hello!" Grandma waved. "Come in and sit

down.'' She served them a special treat of bean cakes. Grandma asked Yoshi many questions, but Mieko sat silently sipping her tea.

Between bites of the light-as-air crispy pastry filled with sweet bean-jam, Yoshi told Grandma all about herself and school.

"My parents were killed when I was a baby," she said, "so I live with my aunt and uncle."

Mieko stared at her in surprise. She had imagined that Yoshi was the luckiest girl in the world who had absolutely everything. She wondered how Yoshi could smile and be nice all the time when she had lost her family.

She accompanied Yoshi to the gate and watched her walk toward home.

In the days that followed, Mieko lingered outside, hoping to see Yoshi again. But she didn't see her until a week later. Mieko and Grandma were buying tea in the grocery shop when Yoshi came in.

"Aunt Hisako sent me for some tea," she told Mieko.

"We came for the same thing," Mieko said, smiling.

They walked together back to Grandma's house.

———

"Would you like to see my room?" Mieko asked shyly.

"Well . . . sure. I guess."

Upstairs, Mieko wanted to show Yoshi something, but she had no special clothes or pretty dolls. She hesitated, then opened a drawer and brought out her four treasures: the inkstone, inkstick, brush and roll of rice paper.

Yoshi ran her fingers over the lily that was carved into the inkstone. Then she stroked the bristles of the brush.

"What fine art supplies!" she exclaimed with admiration. "You must be good at painting."

Mieko did not answer. She put the treasures away. She could not bear to tell Yoshi about how she had lost the fifth treasure. Mieko was sure that Yoshi would not like a girl with so much hatred inside of her.

To change the subject, Mieko took Yoshi to the garden where they puzzled over the words on Grandpa's rock.

As Yoshi was leaving, she asked, "Are you going to school tomorrow?"

Mieko wasn't sure she was ready for school, but she didn't want to say no to Yoshi.

"Maybe."

By suppertime she had made up her mind. Mieko stopped eating her noodle soup and said, "I think I'll go to school tomorrow."

Her grandparents looked up, surprised.

"Grandpa," Mieko went on, her dark eyes serious. "I'm beginning to understand the words on your rock. They mean that I should not worry about my scar, or about going back to school."

He pulled her close to him.

"I do believe you are becoming wise," he said with a chuckle. "You are learning to accept things you cannot change. And most important, you are accepting yourself—scars and all."

After the dishes were washed and put away, they sat and talked—all smiling—until the stars came out.

At bedtime Mieko stared at her face in the mirror. It was plain and round, framed by black hair and bangs. That was all. Mieko wished that a tiny bit of goodness showed in her face like it did in Yoshi's.

This time, as she was falling asleep, there was no sick feeling at the thought of school, and her throat was not so tight. It was as if she was coming into the light after being in a dark tunnel. Maybe everything was going to be all right.

SEVEN

THE
CONTEST

As soon as Mieko entered the classroom, she knew that something was different. Everyone was smiling—except Akira, who scowled at her from his new place in the front row under the teacher's nose.

"We are happy to see you back, Mieko," Miss Suzuki said pleasantly, as if nothing out of the ordinary had happened.

"We've been studying the atom bombs of Hiroshima and Nagasaki," one of the girls said. "You must have been brave."

Mieko felt the bitterness inside of her beginning to disappear like the early morning mist.

After that, school went surprisingly well. Mieko managed to write her lessons with a pencil. Miss Suzuki looked pleased. In composition class, Mieko wrote her first letter home.

> *Dear Mother and Father,*
> *I have a new friend, Yoshi, and I like school.*
> *My hand is still sore, so my writing isn't good. I haven't painted with my brush yet. I miss you, too.*
>
> > *Love,*
> > *Mieko*

One day, in her bedroom, Mieko opened the drawer and brought out her four treasures. Sitting on a cushion, she rubbed the inkstick onto the wetted inkstone. When the ink was black and thick enough, Mieko picked up the brush and began to make the stroke for "one." She felt like a small child learning to write for the first time.

Holding a pencil hadn't hurt much, but a flash of

pain went through her hand when she pressed the brush hard onto the paper. Mieko caught her breath and finished the stroke. She frowned at the crooked line. It didn't look at all like the graceful bone stroke that she had made perfectly countless times before.

Grandma came in and bent over for a look. Mieko tried to cover the paper, but Grandma had already seen the sloppy "one."

"Here." Grandma took the brush and smoothly painted the stroke. "So—that is the way it goes," she said. "Now you try again."

Without a word, Mieko cleaned the brush and inkstone and put the four treasures away. Of course she knew how the stroke should look. Why didn't Grandma know that?

Mieko and Yoshi began spending more and more time together.

"You girls are as close as a pair of chopsticks," Grandpa said.

Sometimes, after school, Mieko took Yoshi to her secret place. Inside the pipe they sat and watched the hermit crabs skittering crazily around on the sand. Or they collected tiny shells, and pebbles worn smooth by the waves.

———

They wandered up the mountain, gathering yellow and gold leaves for Grandma and for Yoshi's Aunt Hisako. Mieko loved the mellow autumn colors that spread over the earth and trees. Often they flung themselves down onto the grass, looking at the sky, trying to find animals in the puffy clouds. Mieko was forgetting the loneliness that used to bring her to the mountain and to the shore.

All the while they kept an eye out for Tengu.

"He has probably gone underground for the winter," Yoshi said with a giggle.

As they raced back down the mountain, they sang,

"Tengu's nose grows and grows.
Tengu's feet——red as a beet!"

The folktale demon became their private joke. During dull history classes they passed notes to each other, adding more lines to their song. Then they hid their faces behind their books and tried not to laugh.

There was a touch of winter in the air when Miss Suzuki made an announcement.

"Our school is having a calligraphy contest on the last day before the New Year's holidays. It will be for those students who paint word-pictures with a brush. At the last minute, I will write the contest word on the blackboard. The one who paints the word with the most artistic brushstrokes will win. Those brushstrokes will be copied onto a brass square and fastened to the big rock in the schoolyard.''

"Let's enter the contest!" Yoshi said eagerly.

Mieko shook her head. How could she think of entering a contest when she couldn't even paint the easiest strokes?

"Please!" coaxed Yoshi. "It will be fun. Besides, none of us had calligraphy lessons during the war, and you studied brush-painting for a long time." She pulled on Mieko's sleeve. "You have a better chance to win than any of us."

"Oh, yes!" Mieko thought bitterly. "I've had lessons, but they are all wasted."

She glanced at Yoshi's delicate fingers. How could she compete against someone like her? And all the others with their perfect hands? Worst of all, Mieko knew that she would never win without the special magic of the fifth treasure.

But Yoshi talked about the contest all the way home and into Mieko's yard. Grandma was washing clothes in a big tub. She lifted a shirt, then slapped it hard against the washboard to get the dirt out. Slap! Slap!

"There's an art contest at school," Yoshi told her, "and I think Mieko should try."

Grandma stopped working, her wet red hands on her hips.

"I think so, too." She looked hard at Mieko. "Your parents would be so proud . . ."

"No!" Mieko said quickly. "I'm not ready." She paused. "I . . . I can't."

And that was the end of it. At least, so Mieko thought.

EIGHT

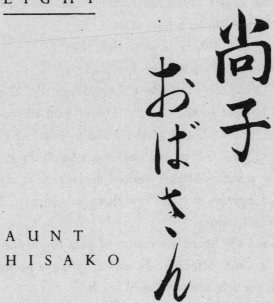

AUNT
HISAKO

One crisp fall day, Yoshi announced, "I'm having a tea party on Sunday. And I want you to come."

Mieko was wildly excited. She was sure Yoshi's house would be like a castle in a fairy tale.

On the special day Grandma did not go out to the fields to help Grandpa harvest rice. Instead, she stayed home to make certain that Mieko was properly

dressed for the important occasion. She tied a blue
ribbon in Mieko's hair, knotting it so tightly that
Mieko yelled. Grandma puffed out the bow and
smoothed Mieko's best skirt.

"Mieko, where is your clean hankie?"

Mieko pulled it from her pocket.

"Don't forget to use it," Grandma said. She gave
one last pat to the dress. "There! You are ready."

At Yoshi's house Mieko stood in front of the tall
closed gate. Off to one side was a small door. After
a few minutes Mieko worked up enough courage to
knock lightly on it. At first there was silence. Mieko
knocked louder.

Soon she heard the clatter of geta inside the yard.

"It's me, Mieko," she called, giving a polite bow
even though nobody could see her.

The small door opened and Yoshi stuck her head
out. "I knew it was you," she said, laughing. "Come
on in."

At the entrance the girls removed their clogs and
donned slippers to walk down the hall. As they flip-
flopped along, Mieko's big slippers kept falling off.
She was glad when they reached the sliding door of
the living room so that she could step barefoot onto
the tatami.

Mieko caught her breath with wonder. The room was so big—eight mats! Silk cushions were waiting near a low table. Mieko's mouth watered when she saw cookies and cakes beside a teapot and matching cups. She hoped they could eat soon.

"Do sit down," Yoshi said in a grown-up hostess voice.

Mieko tucked her feet under her and sat opposite Yoshi. At home she sometimes sprawled, but here she was extra ladylike so as not to shame Grandma.

In the silence the clock on the wall ticked loudly. Mieko looked at the pictures that hung in the alcove and above the door. She liked the black ink dragon best. The artist's brushstrokes flicked and skipped across the paper, making the dragon come alive. Mieko could almost feel the heat from its fiery breath.

The other painting was a poem in calligraphy that said, "In the midst of the world's corruption, a heart of pure white jade."

Mieko wondered what corruption meant.

Suddenly, Yoshi said, "We don't have to be so quiet. It's just us, alone."

Mieko grinned, and soon they were eating the sweets and chattering about school.

———

Mieko had crammed the last cake into her mouth when a slim, elegant woman padded into the room. She was dressed in a green silk kimono with peonies on it and a brocade sash that glittered with gold threads. Her glossy black hair was pulled back into a soft bun.

Mieko stared at her face—so beautiful and smooth, as if she did have a heart of pure white jade.

"Aunt Hisako, this is my best friend, Mieko," Yoshi said.

Aunt Hisako flashed a cool smile in Mieko's direction and lowered herself gracefully onto a cushion.

"When you have finished eating, little stranger, you may call me Aunt Hisako," she said primly. "By the way, young ladies in this house chew each bite thirty times."

While the girls chewed and chewed, Aunt Hisako asked Mieko, "What is your favorite subject at school?"

Mieko had lost count of the chewing, but she was sure that she had done at least thirty, so she swallowed and answered, "The reading class, Aunt Hisako."

Mieko's leg began to go numb and she tried hard not to wriggle. When she could not stand the pins and needles tingling any longer, Mieko sneaked a hand down and rubbed her leg.

Aunt Hisako's eyebrows lifted disapprovingly. She began to talk about calligraphy, using big words that Mieko did not understand.

"Do you paint word-pictures?" Mieko asked meekly.

"Heavens no!" Aunt Hisako replied in her deep voice. "I am only a scholar of brush-painting. In other words, I study the work of famous writing masters. It gives me great pleasure." She fixed her eyes on Mieko. "I suppose you will try to win the school contest, too?"

Mieko shook her head.

"I'm too clumsy."

"Nonsense!" Aunt Hisako threw up her pale hands. "Clumsiness is in your mind. Besides, your hand looks almost completely healed. So that is no excuse."

"But . . ." began Mieko, wondering how best to explain to Aunt Hisako about the lost fifth treasure.

"Little stranger," Aunt Hisako said, "have you not heard of the holy priest, Kobo Daishi, who could paint the most exquisite word-pictures? And not only with his right hand."

———

57

Mieko shook her head.

"With his left hand," Aunt Hisako continued, "or holding a brush between the toes of his right foot, or between the toes of his left foot, or even between his teeth."

Mieko was speechless, trying to imagine what the priest looked like painting with his feet.

"If he can do that, little stranger," Aunt Hisako said sharply, "you can surely paint with one hand."

Mieko shifted uneasily on the cushion, wishing that she had not come. She wondered how long she would have to live in the village before Aunt Hisako stopped calling her a stranger.

"Nothing in life is easy," Aunt Hisako said, rising to her feet. "You don't want to be a coward, do you?"

A coward!

The word thudded inside of Mieko's head. For the first time in weeks the old tightness was back in her throat. She sat there with her head bowed.

"Why don't you look at me?" asked Aunt Hisako. "Do I scare you?"

"A little," Mieko said in a low voice. "But I have seen lots of other frightening things."

Aunt Hisako almost smiled.

———

"So I am a frightening thing?"

Mieko didn't know what to say.

Aunt Hisako turned, saying, "It's time for my nap." As she wafted out of the room she pulled a book from a shelf in the corner. She opened it to show them an illustration, then closed it with a snap that made Mieko jump.

"You may take this book home," Aunt Hisako said. "If you study the brushstrokes on these pages, and practice, one of you might win the prize. Remember, a gem, unless polished, does not glitter."

"Thank you, Aunt Hisako," the girls said in chorus, bowing until their heads almost touched the tatami.

After she left, Yoshi said, "I'm really sorry. Aunt Hisako sounds terrifying, but she only wants to help."

On the way home Mieko thought about what Aunt Hisako had said. She didn't want to be a coward. But how could she try to win the contest without the fifth treasure?

She dutifully told Grandma every detail about Yoshi's grand house and the tea party and Aunt Hisako—everything except the coward part.

But that night she lay awake for a long time. She couldn't forget what Aunt Hisako had said.

As her eyes were closing, Mieko whispered, "I will enter the contest. Even if I have no chance of winning. That will show her I'm *not* a coward."

NINE

友情

FRIENDSHIP

There was one thing about the contest that Mieko did not understand. It buzzed around in her head like a pesky fly all through breakfast.

"You are unusually quiet," Grandpa said. "What's on your mind?"

"Well . . ." Mieko tried to explain. "If two students paint the contest word the same way, who will win?"

Grandpa rubbed the gray stubble on his chin.

"I don't think that is possible," he said slowly. "The wetness, dryness, and speed of one artist's brushstrokes will be different from anyone else's. Painting a word-picture is much like playing the piano. No two expert musicians will play a piece of music in exactly the same way."

He opened Aunt Hisako's book and pointed out some of the masterpieces of calligraphy.

"Here is the word-picture for 'happiness.' It looks quite different when painted by two great artists, doesn't it? They each have a fifth treasure, but their own personalities and styles show up in their work."

Mieko pored over the pages.

"You must paint not what the eye sees," Grandpa said, "but what the heart knows. If your heart has beauty, so will your painting. Do you understand?"

Mieko nodded. "Sort of."

Grandpa smiled broadly.

"Does your question mean that you will enter the contest?"

"Yes, Grandpa," she said, not telling him her reasons.

Grandma turned from the sink. She came over and

---

held out her arms. Mieko buried her face in the clean-smelling apron and hugged Grandma hard.

"That's my brave girl!" Grandma said. "Imagine how proud your parents will be to see your brushstrokes on that brass square!"

Mieko was silent. She wondered if the family would be proud of her even when she lost. Because she surely would.

That same afternoon she and Yoshi began to work on their brushstrokes. Yoshi opened Aunt Hisako's book at the beginning so that they could copy the Japanese word-pictures of the masters.

They sat on their knees with sheets of newspaper spread out on the floor before them. They covered the papers with rows of black strokes. Some were like teardrops, others like mouse tails, stork legs, tiger paws, swords and bones. They made hundreds of them.

Yoshi painted with small, neat, even strokes. But Mieko's were large—thick and thin, fast and slow— sweeping across the page. To make up for the stiffness in her hand, she used her whole body while painting.

While they worked, Mieko told Yoshi stories

about the word-pictures. Her old art teacher had always told stories during class.

"Here are the two parts of the word-picture for house," Mieko said, drawing the strokes. "The first part means 'roof' and the second means 'pig.' "

Yoshi laughed, delighted.

"Imagine putting a pig inside of a house!"

"My teacher said that in the old days people did keep pigs in their houses," Mieko said. "And that is why we draw the word-picture like this."

Yoshi made a face.

"Ugh! Thank goodness we don't have pigs inside anymore."

"And look at this!" Mieko quickly painted the word-picture for "love." "One part means 'woman' and the other stands for 'child,' " she explained. "Put three women together and we get a word-picture that means 'noise.' See?"

"I never thought of that!" Yoshi exclaimed. "But it isn't fair. Three men are noisy, too!"

Between the stories and the practicing, the days flew by.

Soon the rains turned to icy sleet that sounded like thunder on the roof. In the dark, frosty hours after school, Mieko and Yoshi often moved to a low table that had a kotatsu heater underneath it. Grandma had placed a quilt over the table to keep the warmth in. They put their cold hands and feet under the quilt until they thawed out. Then they went back to practicing.

Grandma kept a plate of cookies nearby.

"To keep your strength up," she said, her eyes crinkled in a smile.

She sat beside them with her knitting basket. The steady click, click of her needles made quiet music. Sometimes she shooed Yoshi and Mieko outside for a breath of fresh air and some exercise.

"You must give your eyes a rest," she said wisely.

In their heavy coats, mittens, boots and scarves, they went out into the yard where there was a sprinkling of snow. It glinted like diamonds in the soft light that shone through the paper-paned doors. Even out there Mieko grabbed a stick and made strokes in the snow until Yoshi stopped her.

"This is play time!" she yelled. "I'll race you to the corner!"

Slipping and sliding along the icy road, they shouted their Tengu song.

———

"Tengu's nose grows and grows,
Tengu's feet—red as a beet.
Tengu's paws have awful claws,
Tengu's head—full of lead!"

Weak with laughter, Mieko and Yoshi fell down in a tangled heap of arms and legs.

HOPE

One evening, Mieko was struggling with the difficult strokes for "feast." She tried again and again, but they didn't come out right. Mieko tried thinking about good food—moon buns with bits of pork inside, buckwheat noodles, fried beef and vegetables—until her mouth watered. All at once her brush fairly flew over the paper.

Mieko sat back and studied the word-picture. It was better. The door to her private magical world was opening just a crack. Perhaps a little bit of beauty had crept back into her heart. But would enough of the fifth treasure come back to make the strokes perfect and full of feeling? In time for the contest?

There was only one way to find out. Practice. And Mieko decided to work as hard as she could, even when her hand ached terribly. Then, if the fifth treasure did not return, she would give up calligraphy forever.

Sometimes she turned out two or three almost correct word-pictures in a day. Other times she felt like crying when the strokes were all wrong: the ink was too thick, or too thin, or one stroke was wiggly, or the whole thing was lopsided like a leaky boat.

At bedtime, Grandpa adjusted his glasses and inspected Mieko's practice papers. He held them out at arm's length, then in close for a more careful look. He compared her brushstrokes to those in Aunt Hisako's book.

"Hm-m-m," he said. "That teardrop is too fat . . . the sword must have a sharper edge . . . the elephant's leg should be stronger. And remember that all parts of a word-picture must fit together the way parts of your body fit."

Mieko sagged. It seemed hopeless, but the next day she continued practicing.

The class was growing more excited as the contest drew near. Miss Suzuki asked the artists to bring samples of their painting to school. As the papers were passed around, everyone admired Mieko's large, artistic brushstrokes—even Akira.

"Phew!" he whistled. "I wouldn't work that hard for a million yen!"

He grinned at Mieko and she smiled back. She thought that he really had a nice smile when he wasn't making nasty faces.

However, in spite of the long practice hours, Mieko knew that there was still something missing from her word-pictures.

Even Grandpa agreed.

"Your word-pictures are correct," he said, thoughtfully, "but somehow they seem to lack the spark of life. It is almost as if they were printed by a machine."

Two fat tears squeezed out of Mieko's eyes and rolled down her cheeks. All of her work was for nothing.

"It's no use!" she cried. "The fifth treasure is gone for good."

Grandpa leaned close. "The fifth treasure isn't something you can lose, like misplacing a shoe or sock."

"But ever since the bomb . . ."

Grandpa reached over and wiped away her tears.

"That bomb hurt many people, Mieko. And it hurt your hand. But what's inside of you—the bomb cannot touch that. Perhaps you are trying too hard. The solution might be to give yourself and your brush a rest."

"I can't!" cried Mieko. "The contest is only a few days away."

He cupped her face in his strong hands and looked deeply into her eyes.

"Listen, Mieko dear. You would not be able to dance well if you had just raced a mile, would you? It is the same with calligraphy. You must be fresh to give it your best."

Mieko drew a deep breath.

"All right," she said wearily.

The next day she took a vacation from painting. She tried to put the contest out of her mind and think only about the New Year's celebrations. Mieko helped Grandma clean the house so that every speck of dust would be gone before the next year began.

In the afternoon a letter arrived from home.

Dear Mieko,

I do hope you will enter the contest. The practice will be good for your hand. And I know that the beauty in your heart will again blossom like the peach tree in our garden. Then your brush will feel as though it is dancing across the paper. I'm sure of it—as sure as bamboo bends in the wind.

Love,
Mother

Mieko read the letter many times. She read it in her room and at school. But she was still unsure of herself. She couldn't believe her brush would ever dance across the paper again. Deep down, her worries about the fifth treasure grew.

ELEVEN

THE
TREASURE

The night before the contest, Mieko dreamed that the family was once more together. They were having a picnic under a cherry tree that was blooming like a pink cloud. Mieko was writing a poem about the flowers with her brush. And the word-pictures were full of life.

Gusts of wind began rustling the branches with a whish, whish, whish. When morning came, the sound of rustling turned into a sweeping. Grandma's broom was scraping against the floor of the entrance hall.

Mieko tried to burrow back into her wonderful dream. But it was gone. Shivering in the cold, she hurriedly pulled on her clothes.

She had just gulped down her breakfast when Yoshi came by. Her face was rosy from the cold and the excitement. Yoshi was holding something behind her back.

"Guess what I've got!" she said, hopping on one foot, then the other, trying not to tell the secret.

Mieko couldn't help laughing.

"I can't guess."

"Then close your eyes," ordered Yoshi, "while I take off the wrapping."

Mieko covered her eyes. There was the crackling of paper. Too curious to wait, Mieko peeked. Yoshi was unrolling a sheet of hand-made rice paper.

"Ohhh!" Mieko breathed. She was certain that it was the finest paper made in all of Japan. It was pale cream with a few nubby threads running through. She felt a twinge of jealousy.

———

73

"Wherever did you get it, Yoshi?"

"Aunt Hisako. She ordered it from a store in Tokyo."

"I'm glad for you." Mieko choked out the words.

Yoshi's eyes twinkled when she said, "The paper is not for me." She laughed at Mieko's open-mouthed surprise. "It's for you."

Mieko stood there—stunned—and ashamed of her jealousy.

Yoshi smiled. "You're the one with the real talent, Mieko. My brushstrokes are just plain and ordinary."

"But—" Mieko began to argue. "But you can't . . ."

"No more buts!" Yoshi broke in. "All I want is for you to use this paper. Aunt Hisako said so. Promise!"

When Mieko hesitated, Yoshi stuck out her hand. "Promise!"

Finally, Mieko nodded and they crooked little fingers as they always did to seal a promise.

At school, desks in Miss Suzuki's classroom had been cleared away so that the artists could sit on cushions at low tables. The twenty contestants filed in silently and sat down.

All eyes were on the blackboard where Miss Suzuki would write the contest word.

Mieko's hands shook as she arranged the inkstone, waterholder, inkstick and brush on the table. As she ground the ink, the rhythmic rub, rub, rub calmed her, and she stopped trembling. Then Mieko spread out the soft white paper.

Miss Suzuki wrote the word:

friendship

At that moment the classroom seemed to fade as Mieko concentrated on the word. Inside her magical world—a world where lines and shapes came to life—she saw only the paper and her brush. In her mind's eye she pictured each stroke. Friendship was Yoshi.

All of Mieko's love for her went into the strong, sure brushstrokes. And every one of the fifteen strokes had the energy of a living thing.

Mieko painted the word so quickly that it was as though her hand had been guided. And the brush really did dance across the paper—just as it used to.

Floating in a dream, Mieko put her paper on Miss Suzuki's desk, put on her warm coat, and walked out of the room.

She stood in the quiet schoolyard, the cold air on her cheeks. Happiness washed over her. She had the fifth treasure again. There was no doubt.

Yoshi ran up and grabbed her arm.

"What happened? Why do you look so strange?"

Her eyes shining, Mieko said, "The brush danced. It really did."

"I bet you win!" shrieked Yoshi.

"If I do," Mieko said quietly, "it will be thanks to you. When I thought of friendship, I thought of you. That's what I painted."

Yoshi put her hand on top of the big rock as they walked past it.

"If you win, and your brushstrokes are on this rock," she said sadly, "everyone will always remember you. Especially me." She squeezed Mieko's arm. "I'll miss you a lot."

Mieko blinked away the tears that came when she thought of leaving her best friend.

"When I got here, all I wanted was to go back home. Now it's hard to leave."

"But we can write letters," said Yoshi, brightening. "And maybe you can come back for the summer holidays."

———

"Yes!" cried Mieko. "And we can go to the beach and hide in our secret place . . ."

"And look for Tengu again!" added Yoshi.

They burst out laughing. Then, hand-in-hand, they hurried home through the softly falling snow.

When writing developed in China and Japan thousands of years ago, people did not use letters as we know them but pictures to explain what they meant. The pictures, which today are called "characters," have changed very little over the centuries. They are made up of strokes which, in everyday writing, are produced with pens or pencils. But the Japanese believe that picture-writing with a brush can be great art, and this is the kind of artist Mieko wanted to be.

Many Japanese characters still look almost like what they mean. "Mountain" looks like a mountain:

山

And "tree" looks something like a tree:

木

Other words, like "friendship," are more complicated. The everyday way to write "friendship" is like this:

When painted with a brush, the word-picture looks
like this:

友情

This is how the word-picture looked when Mieko put
her feelings for Yoshi into the prizewinning brushstrokes.